THE
PLAYGROUND
is like the
Jungle

To Sir David Attenborough, with thanks
for guiding us all to see and know.
— Shona Innes

For Palkó and Migi
— Írisz Agócs

FIVE MILE

Five Mile, an imprint of
Bonnier Publishing Australia
Level 6, 534 Church Street,
Richmond, Victoria 3121
www.fivemile.com.au

First published 2017
Printed in China 5 4 3 2

THE PLAYGROUND
is like the
Jungle

Shona Innes * Írisz Agócs

**FIVE
MILE**

The playground is a place
where lots of people come
together to play, and laugh,
and chat and have a break.

Playgrounds can be filled with people
doing their favourite things
with others...

or spending time by themselves.

Playgrounds are a little bit
like the jungle.
Lots of creatures come together
to live and play in the jungle.

And when lots of creatures come together in one spot,

things can get really wild and adventurous.

Creatures have different ways
to make themselves feel good.

They have favourite things
they like to do, favourite
treasures they like to keep,

and favourite creatures
to spend time with.

When creatures feel good they are happy
to share and laugh and play.

And when things don't feel so good,
all creatures have different ways to
take care of themselves.

They have some things they do to hide,

some things they do to scare others away,
and some things they do... just because they can.

People in a playground can be like creatures in a jungle.
There might be some cheeky monkeys chasing
and teasing each other for fun.

Or some big baboons banging their chests, wanting other people to look at them and tell them they're great.

There might be some insects buzzing around,
not realising that they are being annoying...

or tigers that can lash out when they get angry.

There may be some slippery snakes
who pretend to be a friend one moment,

but then just wind away and leave their new friend all alone.

Snakes can be quite good at pretending to be
deaf and not noticing others.

The playground can be fun, but sometimes we can feel very alone.

No one likes to feel alone.

Even though we might feel quite sad and alone sometimes,
there are things we can do to feel happy and safe in the playground.

Some people like to spend time making sure they are
friendly with all sorts of different creatures.

If one creature is giving them a hard time, they have
plenty of other friends they can hang out with.

Some people like to find some things to
do in the quiet part of the jungle.

From here they can relax and spend quiet time alone.

Or they can sit back and have a good look around at what all the other creatures in the jungle are up to, and which ones look like they are safe and happy.

Some people find that even if they are feeling sad and alone, it helps to put on a happy face.

Most other creatures don't want to hang around
with creatures that look miserable.

Some people like to ask for help from the bigger creatures in the jungle.

Asking an adult for help, or playing near adults, can be useful.

Sometimes, if another creature really hurts you,
you need to make a BIG NOISE. This lets all
the other creatures know what has happened...

so that they can come and give you some help,
and so they all know to stay away from creatures that hurt.

Or if someone is really annoying you, you can politely explain how you feel and suggest something else they can do that might make them happy creatures.

Every creature in the jungle is important
to how the jungle works and feels.

The playground can be a bit like a jungle.
It can feel exciting and wonderful.

The playground gives us lots of practice for getting along
with others and learning how to be ourselves.

The playground can be filled with wonderful adventures.